Tales from Plover Cottage

Lisa Woods

Contents

Black Dog   Page   1

The Doctor's Visit   Page   9

In Our Time   Page   17

Treasure Trove   Page   21

The Museum of Rural Life   Page   27

This Guest of Summer   Page   39

1947 – Flood   Page   43

Author's Notes   Page   55

Nothing to Crow About   Page   57

The Comeback King!   Page   65

Mixed Fortunes   Page   73

About the Author   Page   79

Black Dog

First Prize - Wells Literary Festival International Short
Story Competition 2010

Like slipping on a banana skin or falling off a bike it was
an accident waiting to happen. The car clipped the
chevron sign, span round, drifted across the road and
slipped into the drainage ditch. Sitting still for a moment,
she waited for the car to slip further, or some other
catastrophe to follow. Stupid really, she knew how
dangerous this road was. No end of accidents and
fatalities. The car rested, still. Then the engine stalled and
cut out. Shocked but considering herself lucky she
opened the driver's door to look around. Although the
back end of the car was resting in the inky water there
was room for her to clamber out of the door and on to
the steep bank without getting wet. Coat and bag were
on the back seat but reaching over made the car rock and
risked sending it further into the drain. Best to leave
everything. It wasn't that cold after all. Another car
would be along in a moment, someone would stop and
help.

Climbing out of the dyke wasn't as easy as she'd
hoped. With every step the fenland mud oozed around
her feet; the black slub coming above her ankles.
Centuries of plants had gently decayed in the layers of
murky peat, a composting of grass and leaves, festering
dead frogs and newts that all collected as evil muck. With
every step the gases from the rotting mess wafted up with
a smell of decay, old earth and dead breath that hung
around her. Grasping at the clumps of grass helped her
get a purchase to climb the side of the dyke but with each
handful the roots pulled away from the bank, foiling her
attempts. She was stuck half way down this putrid,

mouldy excuse of a drainage ditch. Perhaps there was somewhere where the bank was not so steep, maybe a place where a bridge had been built or machinery left that would give a foothold. Maybe the wreck of a car from a previous accident. Looking along the dyke all that could be seen was yards and more yards of straight, steep bank. Then she saw a shadow moving. A shadow that gradually took on the shape of a dog. A dog trotting along on his own, on the top of the bank.

'Here boy,' she called. The dog came to the side of the bank.

'Come here. Good boy.' How to interest him in staying, on coming closer? Nothing around to encourage him.

'Please come here, good boy. Please.'

The dog lowered himself onto his haunches and looked down at her. His soft skin fell down across his brows, as if he was frowning. As if thinking, 'Now what to do?'

'Come here.' She clicked her fingers at him.

The dog crept forwards, still low, down on his stomach, coming closer. She caught hold of his collar with her right hand and as he leapt backwards trying to get away she held tight and used her left hand to push herself up the bank. Scrabbling with one hand, digging feet into the soft side of the bank, pushing knees into the grass and clinging, clambering, to get to the top of the bank.

The winter dusk was turning to night. Looking across the fields she could see no other cars coming, no encouraging beams of light as people travelled home from work. No lifts to be offered or roadside assistance called. Just fields of black ploughed land that stretched for miles. A flat landscape that was only broken by the dark fringes of reeds where the drainage dykes criss-crossed the land. And far off the lights of a town, away on the horizon. She could see the lantern tower of Ely Cathedral, lit up by spotlights that made it look as though floating above the city, protecting the souls of the residents below. Within sight, but out of reach. Miles away out of reach.

She patted the dog. His coat was silky, groomed and well cared for, he had a name disk but by now it was too dark to be able to read. With his soft coat and gentle snuffling muzzle it was clear that this was no stray. This dog was loved and pampered, with a basket waiting by a hearthside. More importantly, this dog's home probably wasn't too far away. That was it, the best thing to do was to go back with the dog, to his home, and call for help from there.

'Good boy. Go home. Where's home?'

The dog looked up at her, wagged his lazy Labrador tail and then started to trot off.

'Hey, wait for me, wait a minute.' The dog slowed his pace and she walked beside him. Off the side of the dyke, across the tarmac road and down a rutted track made of old broken brick with lumpy grass.

It started to snow, thin little icy balls like polystyrene floating in the air. It was cold without a coat, but it shouldn't be far. The snow wasn't much, just fine dust that swirled round as it fell on the ground. The Labrador walked on, as if he was a modern day St Bernard taking his lost traveller home. Not that far now. The snow melted against her body and left her damp around her cuffs and neckline. The wind that began to whip across the fens lifted her jersey up at the back and she wished she had another layer to stop the cold running up her spine. Head tucked down into her top, she followed the prints left by the dog, trying to avoid looking up into the stinging flakes of snow.

They walked on further, she didn't know for how long. Then looking around her she realised there was no chance of finding an isolated farmhouse out here. There was no sign of life. No welcoming lights in windows, no porch lights left on for late visitors. Just empty blackness that stretched as far as the North Sea. The snow was deeper now, no longer small flurries that eddied around her; now it was large flakes carried by the wind into drifts on the side of the track. The drifts were getting deeper and impeding her way as she struggled along. The paw prints she'd been following as a guide started to disappear under the falling snow as quickly as the dog moved on. It was difficult to see where he was in the dark.

'This is bloody ridiculous. Bloody fine guide dog you've been.' She didn't know whether to feel sorry or angry with the dog. He might be lost too. Probably thought a human would be able to help him. Reaching out to pat the dog she realised she had been mistaken when she thought he was some-one's pampered pooch. His coat was really quite rough, dirty. He was an animal that lived outside in all weathers. His coat was unwashed. He was unfed and unloved. In fact he wasn't a Labrador at all, more of an Alsatian-cross, coarse featured and much bigger than a Labrador. He had lost his collar since she'd used it to pull herself clear of the dyke. Now she'd never know his address to be able to take him back to safety. That's if he had a home.

'Look, you'd best go home. I'm going back. I'll wait by the car.' Even a car in the dyke would be better protection on a night liked this. Stupid to leave it. She might be able to run the engine to get warm.

The dog gave a low growl as she turned around. Hardly audible against the wind, she didn't miss it, and didn't mistake its threat.

'Now then, stop it, you go home now.'

She reached down to see if she could remove her shoe, a sharp slap across the muzzle with that and the dog was bound to run away. The dog leapt forward, snapping with surprisingly large teeth, just short of her face. Protecting herself she turned and started to run, her shoe coming loose as she stumbled down the track. Away from the dog but this meant having to run away from the road. Not the direction she wanted to take but she had to get clear of the dog. Then as she panicked and ran she could see the shape of a shed looming in the dark. The welcoming sight she'd hoped to see. Inside was a blue light, as if people were watching TV with the house lights off. Tumbling down the slope, with the hound still at her heels, hobbling as she ran, she threw herself at the door. The ancient door-knob rattled loose but there were no locks or bolts and the door swung open easily. She fell through into what appeared to be the front room of a tiny cabin.

There were some occupants in the room. Sitting round a table, no TV. Just a gas lamp burning in the centre of the table. The room was palely lit. But even in the half light she could see this was no place to stay. The poor creatures arranged before her were existing in a living death. The odour of centuries of fetid corrosion reached her and she gagged against the smell, recoiling, wanting to escape these new acquaintances. They watched her with eyes that were sunk back in decayed sockets, scarcely able to move or acknowledge her or stretch the fragile sinews that kept their bones together. At the head of the table a Viking, complete with pock marked bronze helmet and grey, wispy whiskered moustache held court. To his right and left were other occupants, a mixed bag of passing strangers who surely had lost their way in times past and were forced to join him at his decomposing banquet. A medieval peasant, with threadbare smock, a Second World War airman with uniform still holding together and beside him the dance-hall girlfriend who, perhaps, spent weeks looking for his body. Only to join him here. On the road to hell.

Feeble and fixed as they were, she could see the fear as their eyes looked over her shoulder, to the monster that now loomed behind her. The dog, huge, black and baying, filled the door space. Standing upright on his hind legs his front claws were talons that clung to the frame. Spittle flew from his foaming mouth, flecking his chest while his eyes flashed with red sparks. He roared at her as she tried to step back to the door and came forward waving his demonic paws. And as she felt herself guided by him, as she turned, it was then that she saw the spare chair at the table. Drawn back waiting for her to join the company.

Her head was on the table, resting. Around her she could hear the murmur of a party, a family party. She had managed to get home after all. Everything was a dream, the awful trek through the snow, and the dreadful timeless dinner party was all some crazy idea that had come into her head while she was resting. There was laughter, voices were raised, shouting and even singing out to one another. As soon as she had the energy she would lift her head, she'd look around and see her mother and sisters. Turning her head to the right she could see the family dog, quietly sleeping in his basket. Tucked out of the way in a corner. His tail wagged as he dreamed in his sleep. Only they didn't have a family dog, did they? Certainly not a black dog, a black Labrador with silky, shiny coat. She raised her head, wanting to smile but full of dread at finding who was at the party she had joined. And there they were, in the full horror of their decrepit state. Her companions tucked away in a fenland shack. Her companions for all time.

The Doctor's Visit

Shortlisted for the Scribble Annual Short Story Competition 2013

Mum didn't let me out to play on the day of the doctor's visit. Instead she did my plaits, told me to put on my gingham dress and then go into the kitchen and lay the tea tray. It would keep me occupied. Mum wasn't happy about the visit, it was all very well the doctor coming out this way but she'd seen enough doctors when Timmy went down to London the first time. While I prepared the tray she went round the front room in her pinny, polishing and dusting everything. Dad was sent out for extra coal, this made him grumpy as he thought the house was quite hot enough already.

I was happy preparing the tray. It was a treat to handle the bone china that was normally kept away in Mum's cupboard. It was the first time I'd been allowed to touch the best set with its red and yellow roses and real gold rims. After carefully wiping the cups and saucers I warmed the teapot, leaving it to stand on the draining board while I boiled the kettle.

Dad was first to see the visitor's car coming down the lane. 'The bugger's in a Rolls Royce,' he said.

I could see the black car bumping across the ruts with two men sitting behind the chauffeur. Running around the kitchen table to get a better look I bumped into the tray and in an instant the teacups slid over the edge and tilted the tray sending it crashing down. As the cups hit the floor I could only watch helplessly hoping that they wouldn't break but the china was delicate and the quarry tiles were hard. The cups became fragments of flying roses.

Mum dragged me away from the kitchen and across the room to stand by the front door. There wasn't time for her to say anything, but from the way she pinched my arm I knew that I'd hear about this later.

'Don't offer them any tea,' she said to Dad, pulling the kitchen door behind her to hide the smashed china.

Through the front window I could see the car arriving and was cross to see Andy, from next-door, run up as the car stopped outside our house. You would have thought they were visiting him, not us. He ran up just like he lived here and stood to attention as if the King was in the car.

Two men stepped through the front door filling the whole room as they arrived. I felt I had to stand against the wall to give them space to move. They took their hats off but the smaller man kept his coat on. The bigger man had a fat tummy and I could see that under his jacket he had braces that curved around to be able to meet his trousers.

'Now, where's the patient?' the big man asked. He smiled but his loud voice frightened me, like it was too large for the room as well.

Mum brought Timmy across to him. Our little lad was wearing his red dressing gown, the one he'd been given in the hospital. The big man, who must have been the doctor, removed the gown and Timmy stood before him shivering in his woollen underwear. Pulling the vest up the doctor took a stethoscope in his fat white hands and placed it against Timmy's chest. The doctor listened to Timmy's left side and then moved the stethoscope over to his right.

'Well, I say.' He smiled over to his companion. 'Have a listen to this, *situs inversus viscerum*. Doctor Smithson was correct it does seem to be the inverted position of the internal organs.'

The other man stepped quickly over to Timmy. He had a funny sort of smile, his lips were pursed up, as Dad would say 'like he'd swallowed a bee'. He still hadn't taken his coat off and had to remove his gloves and rub his hands before he took the stethoscope. Timmy flinched as he was taken by the shoulder.

'Sorry old chap, a bit cold in here. Sorry about the cold hands. Stand still a minute.'

I looked over at Dad. I was surprised that the man was cold after Dad had been saying all day that the room was much too hot. He kept looking straight ahead of him, as if he'd rather be outside, perhaps in the garden or on the farm.

'Good Lord,' said the man smiling at the doctor. 'Astonishing.'

He turned Timmy and started to push his sides and then placed his hands against Timmy's ribs.

He looked at the doctor and continued speaking to him, 'Pity you missed seeing him when they brought him down to London you know. Good thing you were coming over to Newmarket to see the races.'

'D'you know, I think we'd like him to come back down to London,' said the doctor, speaking to Dad now. 'He really is an interesting case. I wonder if all his organs are round in reverse. Remarkable.'

'And what would you do there?' asked Dad in a low voice. 'Operate on him?'

'Well quite likely, yes, but not that we can do anything. We'd be able to see if it is just *situs inversus with dextrocardia* or perhaps *situs inversus with levocardia*. You see sometimes it's just the heart that's on the right side of the body and sometimes it's all the organs are reversed.'

'Oh, very interesting. And just what good would that do?' Dad's voice was muffled. He had his chin pressed almost against his chest while his eyes were looking down at the floor.

'Well just sometimes, when it's the heart only, we find other things that are wrong, other congenital defects.'

Dad looked up sharply. 'And what would conning whatsit defect be when it's at home?'

'There from birth,' said the doctor, standing up. 'Of course we wouldn't be able to do anything, can't change something like this old man.' The doctor gave Timmy's head a pat.

Mum was crying and I rushed over to pull Timmy close to me, to put his dressing gown back over his shoulders. I looked at Mum but she just kept on crying, rubbing her hands over her apron. I looked at Dad to see if he might speak but he didn't seem to want to say anything either. For a horrible moment I thought of them taking Timmy away and of him lying alone in a hospital. This time no one would be able to afford to stay.

'You're *not* to take him,' I shouted. 'You're not kind and you're not nice. You're *not* to take him.'

Dad looked so mad I thought he was about to come across the room and thrash me for that and I knew he would still be cross about the tea set. I wasn't half going to catch it in a minute. Instead he turned to face the doctor.

'I think she's right don't you? You haven't come here to make him better, you're just curious, nosey parkers. My son's not going off to be a peep-show freak and he certainly isn't ending up on your slab. Just a bit of entertainment after your day at the races. You might be offering free treatment but I don't think we need it thank you. You're not going to make him any better. So we'll stick with what we've got here if that's all the same to you.'

He bent down and picked up the doctor's hat and passed it to him, then walked across the room and opened the door for them both to leave. The doctor waved his hat at Mum as a farewell and walked to the door with the other man following silently.

As they got in the car I saw the doctor give Andy a coin. The car drove off and Andy had to jump out of the way as a spray of muddy water splashed out from under the wheels.

I looked at Mum to see what was coming, but she seemed to have forgotten me, she was sitting on the armchair cuddling Timmy. Dad was already at the back door pulling on his work boots. I ran up to change and then outside to play. When I was out playing I asked Andy about the coin I'd seen the doctor give him.

'It was a tanner,' said Andy. 'But me mum took it, said she needed it more'n me.'

He smiled, showing his little gappy black teeth. Sixpence, that was a lot. I was glad they'd got something; they were a poor and dirty family. I wouldn't have wanted that doctor's money in any case. As Dad said before he went back to work, we were all well shot on 'em.

That's a long time ago now, before the war and the National Health Service. Despite what the doctor said our Timmy grew up to be a fine young man. When war came he was quick to sign up. How it broke Mum's heart that day.

But Tim said to her, 'I can't stay at home while other men are fighting'.

He was away a long time, he saw action in the desert and Italy, and he returned home to us injured. The sniper that shot him had a good aim but you see, he didn't know what the doctor had told us that day, so he accurately hit Tim's left side. With his heart on the other side of his body this was a serious injury for Tim but not fatal. He was saved for us by a miracle. Back home with us he recovered, in time, and went on to have a good life.

As Dad would say, saved for us by that there congenital whatsit.

In Our Time

First Prize Winner - Inaugural Ely Writer's Day
Short Story Competition 2015

My grandsons are playing on the lawn. They circle Louise and the baby, whooping in delight, spraying water from their plastic guns. The baby girl leans forward and squeals at them, little hands clasping and feet kicking in excitement. It's a beautiful summer day and my garden is looking its best. I wonder for how long. But after all that's what a visit to Granny's is all about, having lots of space and being treated to the things they've always wanted.

My cat makes the mistake of jumping down into the garden from the neighbour's fence. I'm surprised he hasn't heard the singing and shouting. Too late, he realises that there are visitors, but not before a spray of water has hit him. It's surprisingly accurate, leaving a furrow of fur that ends in a quiff between his ears. Disgusted he heads for the tree before there's a second shot. The boys are after him but, knowing where he's going, he disappears up into the leafy branches.

I'm watching this from the kitchen unable to do more to help the unfortunate feline. Drinks for the boys are already outside and I have come in to prepare squash for Louise and myself. I feel in need of something stronger.

'It's lovely to see Louise and the children here.' It's my husband, Paul, who's crept up on me. 'Has Ben come with her?'

'No,' I reply. 'He's like you used to be, too busy to get away from work.'

'If I'd known what I know now, I'd have spent more time with you all,' he replies.

'I know. We always missed you.' I don't want to dwell on this, now's not the right time for sad reminiscing and 'what ifs'.

'They're beautiful children.' He's looking through the window. 'What a gorgeous little girl.' He chuckles. 'She'll be a handful if she ever catches up with them.'

'Tell me about it.' I pause for a moment. 'From what Louise says I wouldn't be surprised if they decide to go for another one.'

The ice is melting in our drinks. I'd prepare something for him, to stop him from leaving, but he doesn't need a drink. I don't want him to go, not just yet. He starts to move towards the door and I can't think of anything else to say that will keep him.

'See you later?' I ask.

He nods, 'I'll be waiting for you.'

And he's gone. I pick up the tray and carry the drinks to the garden. Paul died four years ago. For a while he visited me frequently but not so much now. Time moves differently on the other side and it's hard for him to know that our lives have moved on without him. I expect he picked up the happiness of children singing and it brought him home for a short while. I wipe my eyes, fix a smile and walk out into the dazzling sunlight.

Treasure Trove

If you stand in one place long enough you can watch the seasons change around you. The sun-splashed green of an English spring turns to the tawny gold of summer. During the long winter months the ploughed brown fields of hills, concealed by verdant leaves in the summer months, can be seen through the bare black branches of sleeping trees.

Turn and it is spring, turn again and it is autumn. Autumn was the season when he'd met her with her hair golden, glowing in the mellow sun. He turns again and then it is spring.

'Ain't you tired of that yet?' They always ask him. They don't understand what makes him come here. They think that by now he could give up on that lark. Or at least find somewhere else to go.

He's been coming here for years. First off he came here to get away from his family. He'd enjoyed the solitude of north Norfolk, and had stayed at a small pub in a nearby seaside village. It was at the pub where he'd met the farmer who had agreed to him metal detecting on this estate. The ground was sandy, with a bit of flint riding through it. The farmer grew wheat on the land but it wasn't much good for root crops as the soil was thin. He was careful when the crops were young; as the wheat grew he kept to the edges of the field. With the soothing hum of the machine purring through his headphones he would happily sweep the loop of the metal detector over the ground. Scything across the land, gleaning small pleasure, absorbed in the repetition of the task.

It was here at this spot where he'd first seen her, though he hadn't seen her coming. Suddenly, her face was next to his; green eyes looking at him, a big grin about to turn into giggles. He didn't catch what she said, even when he removed his earphones but he understood well enough what she was asking.

'Here, course you can have a go,' he said, handing her the headphones

She placed the 'phones on her ears, as he had been wearing them, and then collapsed laughing. He'd moved the machine around to change the range of the beeps in the hope it would keep her interested. She had spoken to him but he didn't quite get the dialect. He thought perhaps she might be Scottish, what with the auburn hair and her clothes. He didn't know that much about women or the fashions they wore. Maybe she was wearing what they called 'retro', with a shawl, long skirt and sandals.

She'd handed the headphones back and left, walking down the track with her hair flashing bright sparks in the sunshine. He watched her walk past a small spinney of trees before going into the denser wood on a hill across the road. After a while he thought he'd follow the route she'd taken. Down the flinty track, across the tarmac road and into the woods. He reached the calm of the trees and the scent of the pine mingling with the peat soothed him. These were earthy, ancient smells.

The path he was on was steep and difficult to climb, he realised that she probably hadn't come this way after all. In fact, it looked as though no-one had been this way for a long time. The path was just about passable, it was an old track, but there were no recent footprints and no sign of maintenance. There were small landslides where the hill had eroded into small cliffs. Oh well, he'd thought, while he was here he might as well do some detecting.

And that was where he'd found the hoard. Gold that held the warm glow of summers from two thousand years ago. Gold that had lain below the soft peat waiting for the return of its owners. The gold of torcs, bracelets, shawl pins, combs and brooches all packed away just under the topsoil. This wasn't the gold seen under a jeweller's bright lights, lucre that flashes its tempting outrageous extravagance. This was the gold of tradition, religion and love. These were items placed carefully by a long lost people, fleeing from an avenging army. People who had not intended to stay away from their homes but who were never able to return. Not in their lifetimes.

He was later told by the museum curators that the items had been hidden by the Iceni tribe. These were a proud people who had raised the wrath of the Roman Empire through the massacre and burning of Colchester. It was this tribe that went on to attack St Albans and London. The Romans, ferocious at the bloodthirsty violent damage to their towns and people, had brought in their own troops to hunt the Iceni down. The tribe were believed to have fled into the swamps and mud of the Fens. Across Norfolk small finds of their lost treasure continued to be made. The collection he'd found that day was the largest ever recorded. Treasure trove rules applied.

Now he stayed at a different pub, it cost a bit more but that wasn't a problem. The food was good and what he really liked was the private seating in the restaurant. High backed ancient oak pews had been converted into booths allowing privacy from other parties. After his evening meal he liked to finish with a whisky then head back to his room before the crowded bar started to disperse with people milling around the door and staircase, his exit. While he was sitting, tumbler in hand, he noticed another diner. It was a woman with bright red hair that fluffed around her head and lay in long locks down her back. The gorgeous colour flashed like the sparks of the log fire and reflected the colour of the flames that blazed up the blackened chimney. He knew her immediately as the girl he'd seen before.

He moved to a quieter space. In the hallway, between the door and the stairs were a couple of wooden chairs. He sat on one and watched her walk past the crowded bar and into the hallway. Just like last time she was in a shawl and long skirt down to her ankles. No-one else in the room seemed to notice her. She walked up to him, lightly touched his shoulder and then, with the briefest of smiles, walked away from him. He'd lost her again. He took the stairway to his room and prepared for an early night.

The sound on the TV was low as he lay on the bed. The comforting glow of a bedside lamp enhanced the cosiness of this guest room. He was angry with himself that he'd blown his one chance of striking up a conversation with the woman. Then he heard a light knock on the door. Room service was not an option here and there were no other guests. This intrusion was a surprise to him. Still partly dressed he opened the door to the woman he had dreamed about for so long. She pushed the door aside and without any invitation entered, slamming the door behind her. This wasn't the laughing golden haired young woman he'd met so long ago. This woman, who entered bare-breasted with arms raised, was a shrieking monster. She strode wailing into the room. Her howl was the cry of lost hope, murder and theft. The blue and purple images blazoned across her strong arms and shoulders leapt as she lashed out at him. The stuff of nightmares had arrived.

The lamp beside his bed continued to share its warm glow, but the shadows from it that danced on the far wall told a tale of dark, violent terror. Reaching desperately for sanctuary, he turned and saw his own macabre silhouette. The shadow of a crouching man with a woman's arm raised above him, her hair flowing back. He turned again to see her lift a dagger and launch forward with a deadly thrust. A lunge that was aimed to slice him from hip to throat, as it did so many Romans in the past. The quiet man had no time to shout or call for help. The stabbing disembowelled him and left his blood to run across the pale carpet of the immaculate tourist accommodation.

The dagger will not be seen again, it is the one that still remains hidden in a Norfolk wood, the dagger that all his detecting had failed to find. A weapon that belongs to another, other world. It is the blade that cuts with a speed that leaves no time for a cry. This wrath of the brave feted, and defeated, Boudicca is the last killing.

As sure as season follows season, violation is followed by retribution, and after two millennia Boudicca avenged the last and final theft from the Iceni. The tribe who left, never left.

The Museum of Rural Life

Charles

I'm running along the field edge, scaring birds. I have a stick with a piece of rag attached. It's a flag. I'm at Sevastopol. Like my father I'm fighting the Russians.

The gang are working at the far side of the field. They're gleaning the last of the wheat. Today they'll finish work on the harvest. I'm not sure what they'll start tomorrow. It's my job to scare the birds so that they can't eat the last of the wheat before we can gather it in ready to sell.

The black birds fly off as I run along. I'm with the Light Brigade.

'Chaaarge,' I shout as I get near to them. The birds hang in the air, like spirits, as I go past. Afterwards they fall to the ground and strut back around the field. I pick up a stone to throw at the birds. I'm quite a good shot. The birds fly into the air again. When they settle on the ground they are out of my reach.

I've got a collection of stones. I keep them in a hollow at the far end of the field. I go there when the gang is working near the orchards. I'm building a stack of pebbles. It's quite difficult, I have to arrange the order carefully or else the pebbles fall down. One stone I keep separate from the others. It has a hole in the centre, it's a special one.

I'm near to the hedge where we ate our docky. I had an apple with my bread today. It was very nice; we don't always have apples. I collect the cloths we had our dockies packed in. I arrange them neatly. Really I'm looking to see if there are crumbs or if anyone has left any food, but there's nothing. I'm hungry. I lie down as I'm so hungry. I think the best thing is to have a sleep.

Rebecca

I can see the child sleeping by the hedge. He'll be tired; he's been running around all day. Sometimes he's out of sight, he goes down in the corner of the field where I can't see him. I become afraid that vagabonds might attack him. I'm not sure what he's got down there. I hope he's not still sleeping when Richard comes back. Richard will accuse him of laziness if he finds him sleeping, but he's not lazy he's just tired after running around scaring the birds.

We've nearly finished the work on this land. When I arrived in the spring we worked on emptying the cattle barns. Then we spread muck and helped the ploughman. Now the crops are harvested. I don't know what Richard will ask us to do in the winter. I hope the work won't be as hard.

I can see Richard approaching now. The lad is awake and has picked up his stick. He knows how important it is to look busy when the gang-master is around. Richard stops to speak to him but I don't think it's unkindly as the lad starts to skip as he waves the stick.

'You can knock off now.'

Richard will be in a rush to get us back to our home, he doesn't like to hang about when he comes to collect us. We put the last of the wheat into a sack and carry the sack over to the wagon that's waiting with the rest of the load.

After that we collect our belongings and fall into file behind Richard. We walk back along the track to the sheds where we sleep. The boy has been barefoot all afternoon but I make him put his boots on for the walk home. The boots are tight to wear but his feet will hurt more if he walks shoeless on the flint path.

Richard brings our evening meal round as soon as we're back home. He offers me a bowl of thin soup.

'That's not enough Richard,' I say.

'Mr Dack t'you, if you remember,' he says.

I find it hard to call him 'Mr', as if he were my better. Normally he lets me call him by his first name. There's something wrong. The food isn't what we usually receive and he's angry with me.

'It's not enough to feed the child food like this.' I try to explain.

'Yon child dursn't do enough work for more food,' he grunts back.

The boy does as much as he can. In the spring they were happy to feed him for chasing the birds and lifting out stones from the land. Now that we're coming into the winter they're changing their minds.

'But he's growing, he needs better food.'

'All more reason for 'im to do proper work then. If 'e wants food 'e'll 'ave t'work with the cattle.'

We both know this work will be too hard for the lad. I look at Richard and see no reaction in his face, no care or interest. He's telling me what his mother, Mrs Dack, has decided. Charles will either have to work with the cattle or go without food. It's clear they don't want us here, not now winter's coming and the work is becoming scarce.

I take the soup; it has a greasy film floating on the surface with a few shredded cabbage leaves in a thin watery stock. Richard pulls some bread out of his pocket and offers me that too.

We sleep on some sacks and the next morning, when the gang next door starts to rise, I stay on the bed and let Charles sleep. They don't think much of me. The women are bitter when they see Charles. They tell me I must be a fool to have the child, that I should have done what a lot of women have done, I should have killed my child at birth and saved myself the hardship of raising him on my own.

Richard comes to the door and I get up to speak to him.

'We're leaving Richard, we can't stay here if you won't feed us.'

I don't get a reply, just raised eyebrows. Then he goes next door to collect the rest of the gang. They follow him out. I wonder where they will work today. Already there is sharpness to the air. Winter will soon be here and the gang will be working in the freezing mud. I'm not staying here to freeze and starve.

There's no food to offer Charles. He was so hungry the night before I allowed him all of the bread. It's going to be hard for him to walk far without anything to eat. Then Richard turns round and comes back to me. He reaches into his pocket and brings out some bread. I think it might have been there since last night, but I'm not too proud to take it. I hand the food to Charles and have the satisfaction of watching him eat.

We are lucky. As we leave the yard the carter goes by with his horse. He asks if we're going far and when I reply he offers to let us ride on the back of the cart. It's a generous offer as he doesn't have to make his horse pull the extra weight, but I suppose we are only two small ones extra to the load of wheat he's already pulling.

The cart jolts and bounces along the rutted drove. It's baked hard at the moment, but that's better for the horse than pulling through mud which will come soon enough. We make good time. It's only mid-afternoon when we reach our new home. The carter sets us down outside the large metal gates.

'I suppose it's better for you and the little'un,' says the carter.

He's right. I've tried to avoid this but now I've come to see that it's the best thing for us both. We wave good-bye to the old man and his kind horse. Then we enter through the gate at the side of the imposing double gates and cross over to the front door. Here there is a smaller door to the side, I ring the bell and wait for an answer.

The person who arrives is friendly enough.

'Coming in?' she asks. I nod.

We enter a hallway, there are three doorways leading from this room. There's a pile of clothing, grubby white smocks.

'The little'un can take one of those,' advises our guide, 'and you can have one of these.' She offers me a dark blue dress; it's made of coarse wool that will be uncomfortable to wear.

I put the smock over the head of the lad. He immediately appears fragile and smaller.

'He needs to go through that door,' she nods her head to a door on the right, 'and you'll be going through that one.'

The lad hasn't realised what's happening, he's being guided towards the door by another servant. I turn to one of the doors on my left, just as he begins to understand where we are.

As I push the door and enter the female block on my own I hear my child start to scream.

Charlie

'What's this place?'

We've parked outside a large house. There are some massive gates and a gravel area where we've parked our car. I'm not very impressed.

'The museum of rural life,' Mum answers.

'You mean this is where we've come for a day out? Like we could have gone to the beach or park, but nooo, we've come to a skanky museum.'

I look round, I can't see any children here, just really old people walking about. Well you'd have to be really old to want to come to a museum when the schools are on holiday.

'Come on,' says Mum, 'let's have a look at least. There are farm animals and things, I'm sure you'll like it.'

I hand her my i-pad which she puts in her bag. Then I get out of the car. Oh, and it's really smelly here, like yuck, there must be a farmyard.

We go through the large wooden doors into a hallway. There's some clothes on hangers. White things, and a few navy dresses. Like, really boring. Mum tells me that when people come on school trips they use the outfits to dress up. So they can pretend to live here. Oh, base.

Mum pays the entrance fee then starts to read all the little label thingies to find out about the place. Well I can tell you it's horrible and smelly, so who needs to know anything more. After a while she agrees to go outside. I think we could look for somewhere to get a drink and then I'll go on my i-pad.

There's a little field full of trees. Small trees, not very high, all in rows. The field has a stone wall all the way round. I have a look inside and see the first kid I've found since getting here. He's a bit pale and scrawny but he's probably alright. I run over to see if he'd like to play. I've got a football in the car if we need one.

The boy looks a bit younger than me, but he's alright. As soon as I run over he starts running too. We chuck a couple of apples off the trees at each other and then I think of a really crazy game where I crash against the wall and pretend to be injured. The boy follows this game and does the same thing. He's laughing and I'm laughing. He's a really funny bloke.

Becki

It's not easy knowing what to do in the summer holidays. Some of Charlie's friends have gone off on holiday but we're having a staycation this year. Now that I'm on my own I've got to watch the money. I thought the museum would be a good idea but Charlie started being really difficult as soon as he got here.

He does look as though he's enjoying himself now though. I'm not sure what he's doing, running around like an idiot but at least he's stopped pestering me. I must admit I hadn't realised what the museum was until I got here. It didn't mention on the publicity material but it's an old workhouse. Been here for two hundred years. It's giving me the shivers. I know what these places must have been like, I could never get over the fate of Fanny Robin in 'Far from the Madding Crowd'. The poor people who ended up here, separated from their loved ones, not even allowed to stay in the same dormitories.

As Charlie is running round the orchard I go over to read a plaque near the gate. I feel my blood run cold. It might be pretty with the red apples showing against the green leaves, but in this area are buried the residents of the workhouse. They were buried as paupers here among the apple trees. After they arrived here at the workhouse they never got away again.

'C'mon Charlie,' I call, 'let's go and see the animals in the farmyard.'

Charlie looks away from me as if he's talking to someone.

'There's only pigs, Mum,' he shouts to me. 'All the other animals are miles away in the fields.'

I tell him to come on. We can look at the animals and then I'll see if we've got time to get to the beach. I'm feeling depressed here, I need to get away quickly.

Charlie follows me, and he's right, there are only pigs. They're not very nice, they are a bit smelly after all. Charlie looks frightened of them.

'He says they bite Mum,' he tries to explain. Who says they bite I've no idea, but they're certainly not entertaining. Then I realise that Charlie's making up an imaginary friend. I'm quite shocked, it's not something he's done before and he's a bit old for all that now. It must be because he's lonely, having to come out for the day without any friends from school.

'Oh come on Charlie,' I say. 'You're right it's been a mistake coming here. Let's go, we can go to a McDonald's on the way home if you like.'

We go back to the car. There aren't many people in the car-park. I suppose people have got more sense than to come here. I open the windows to let some air in.

'Charlie, get in will you.'

Charlie opens one of the back doors but instead of getting in he runs round to the other side and opens the back door. It's like he's helping someone get in. All polite and helping with seat belts and everything. Play acting for attention. Then he runs back and climbs in to the seat behind me. The car doors slam shut one after the other. I don't know how the far one could have closed as Charlie had already fastened his seat belt. Charlie laughs and gives a thumbs up sign.

'Charles says he's glad he's leaving this place and coming home with us,' says Charlie. 'He says he never did like it here, neither.'

This Guest of Summer

Highly Commended – Ely Writers Day 2016

This guest of summer,

The temple haunting martlet does approve

By his loved mansionry that the heavens' breath

Smells wooingly here.

(Macbeth 1.63 – 1.66)

Duncan surveyed the room approvingly. It was the first time he'd visited Mac's home and he was pleased to see how well the décor reflected the man he had come to know. A few years ago Duncan had laughed that you could take the boy out of Glasgow but never Glasgow out of the boy. Now he could see he'd been wrong. In this room modern ideas mixed easily with traditional. On the walls were sepia photos of Mac's family. Prints of the thistle image were reproduced not in some touristy or arty manner but tastefully in a subtle way. Making a statement only to those who would be aware of it, and in the know.

Even more impressive, it was a pretty house; and that wasn't something you could say about many houses in Aberdeen. Yes, it was a lovely setting with birdsong outside and sun shining through the windows.

Duncan thought that a man who had achieved so much over the years deserved to see the benefits for his family. And it was all paid for with oil money. As Duncan had said before 'oil money is good money, there's plenty of it around and more where it came from'.

He looked across the table at the other guests. All captains from his own industry. Good men that he trusted well; almost as much as he trusted Mac.

There were great aromas coming from the kitchen where the hosts were busy preparing lunch. A celebratory feast.

"Screw your courage."

The words, spoken in the kitchen by his honoured hostess, were plainly heard and Duncan felt the first jolt of unease. He had hoped for harmony, not strife.

Mac walked into the room. The rising star who had conquered negotiations at Fife, Norway and the Western Isles. Difficult transactions, that had taken skills to resolve, but now the oil was flowing freely again. Duncan looked to his man, and caught something from his look that made the cold clutch at his throat. Too late he understood the nature of the late night meetings he had sent Mac to attend on his behalf. Meetings that should have favoured Duncan. Now he knew these meetings had allowed Mac to become a usurper. Duncan's time had come and Mac was the one ready to discard him.

Like a dagger floating between him and Mac he recognised the threat he was facing. He stood and held his glass out in a toast to his companions.

'To Banquo, may you beware the rooky wood; and Macduff, don't travel too far from your wife and babes, never forget your pretty ones.'

Sadly, he looked towards Mac.

'Mac, beware your vaulting ambition, do you but not think it o'erleaps itself today?'

Duncan knew all was lost, the deed was done.

'Ay', he said softly to his host. 'Lay on, Macbeth.'

1947 - Flood

Short-listed - Strand's International Short Story Competition 2017

'Ferryman!'

Sam wasn't of a mind to rush and answer the knock at the door. He didn't really take to his customers summoning him like this. When he was ready he opened the door and felt the full force of the gale blow in. The wind was enough to snatch the door from him but he held on tight. He could see a tall form in front of him.

'Who the effing 'ell is calling round at this time of night?' he asked.

'That's no way to speak to a servant of the Crown,' came the reply. Sam now saw that the height of the fellow was due to him wearing a policeman's helmet. Although Sam knew most of the Bobbies around here this wasn't some-one he'd come across before.

'I need you to row me across the causeway,' announced the visitor.

'On a night like this? You must be joking.'

Rain was lashing down. So heavy that, as it came down, it completely missed the guttering and streamed straight to the ground. It hadn't stopped raining for days and now there was just mud and puddles outside the door. Something loose was banging in the fierce wind.

'I need you to take me across the causeway,' repeated the policeman, 'as there's a criminal we need to question residing in a house on the other side. I need to apprehend him.'

'You have no bleeding idea how dangerous it will be out there tonight,' replied Sam. 'The water's over six foot deep and the flow on that flood in this gale will carry us down to Denver.'

'All the same … you can say what you like,' replied the constable, 'but you're going to take me over.'

Taking a moment to find his waterproofs Sam pulled on a large cape, hat, waders and gauntlets. Then he led the policeman round to the mooring. His wooden boat was straining at the mooring rope, pulling away with every gust of wind. Sam drew the boat towards him, the rope would be wet so he kept the gauntlets on, he would remove them as soon as he started rowing. He pulled the boat alongside the small quayside and signalled to his customer to climb on board. The boat was bobbing around like a lost moorhen and the policeman wasn't that nimble as he climbed down into the boat. He slipped a little as he tried to find the seat and for a moment sat down in the bilge. He'd get a wet arse thought Sam, smiling.

Sam pulled the gauntlets off and chucked them over on the bank. He wouldn't need them now as he'd want to keep a hold of the oars, with the rain and river water he couldn't afford to slip his grip. He had the rope looped around a post as he sorted himself out and prepared for the journey. It would be nearly a mile across the flood and would take a good half hour. He pulled the boat around a little, using the rope, then he let one end go as he swung the front of the boat quickly round. The current caught and swept the boat along with it for a moment while Sam grabbed the loose rope. He neatly rolled it up and placed it tidily away. After that he dug the oar deep into the water and took control. His plan was to row into the flood, heading up stream. Then he would let the current carry them most of the way across as he pulled more on the right oar to keep the boat from floating too far down stream and away from the jetty on the other side.

The policeman was keeping surprisingly quiet after all the fuss he'd been making on dry land. Sam thought he was probably surprised to find himself so low down in this little boat. Mostly people did find that they were a lot nearer to the water than they'd expected when they made the crossing.

It was a good job that there was a moon tonight. Sam was well used to the route but even so when things were in full flood it was easy for branches and even trees to suddenly come sweeping down. Add to that, you had to avoid the bushes and trees that grew along here when there wasn't a flood and all in all it was a bit perilous.

'Reckon I'll stop over at the George tonight,' Sam said. He was trying to start a conversation so that it could help take his mind off the rowing. He was used to the work, but tonight it was hard as he had to pull against the flood. Underneath his oilskin cape he was sweating, he'd soon be as wet inside as out. His companion didn't comment. He looked well frit.

It was a dangerous night to be out but Sam had been rowing across these waters since he was twelve so he didn't really have any fear for this work. He'd have rather been at home in front of the fire but he was a ferryman like his father before him and his father before that. Just dig in deep and you'll soon be across. Sometimes you could row over and the oars would gently splash as they entered the water and you were almost sculling, but tonight it needed some effort. It wasn't possible to hear the oars, the gale was blowing and the howling of the wind covered any other noise. As they approached the jetty he could see the properties that stood on the road alongside. A police car, lit up by the interior light, was parked outside one of the houses.

'Is that where you were expecting to find your felon?' asked Sam.

A couple of men in police uniform were leading another man out from the front door of the house.

'Looks like you've missed them,' continued Sam. 'You should have gone with your mates and driven round the right side of the water, you'd have been in time then.' He pulled the boat close to the jetty, there were some steps and the policeman climbed out. 'If I were you I'd grab that spare seat in the car and save myself from crossing back over. Your car will be safe in the village until tomorrow and you can come and fetch it then.'

Still without saying anything to Sam, the police officer headed over to the car. He opened the back door and got in just before the vehicle moved off.

Whether to stay at the pub or not. The outside light was on but there didn't seem to be much activity. Not surprising really if the coppers had been round. Most of the drinking crew were probably holed up in there with the lights out. A drip of water ran down the back of his neck. Sam shivered and drew his shoulders up tighter round his ears. Best head back really. He could get his wet stuff off at home. If he stayed here the night he'd only have wet things to put back on tomorrow. He gave the boat a shove away from the jetty and then thought of the best way to get back.

He didn't have much time to think. Although there had been a steady flow on the water as he'd travelled across it hadn't been that difficult to manage but now it was as if a mighty plug had been pulled out of a giant bath. The water was forcing itself all around him. Swirling and pulling, the water started to carry the boat along. Whatever Sam did to try and control it the water just seemed to push the boat on more wildly. The boat was bucking over the water like a wild thing. It would have been easier with another body on board to keep the vessel lower in the water but with just one the little boat was left to skip and lift helplessly. Sam did the only thing he knew to do. He dug the oar down deep into the water and tried to bring the boat round, but in doing that the worst possible thing happened and the oar slipped away from his grasp. Sam tried helplessly to catch the oar just as it went loose but too late, and in an instant the oar disappeared out of his hand and into the deep water. All that was left now was for the boat to spin around like a dog endlessly chasing its tail.

Betty hadn't expected Sam to be back from the crossing. He would often stay over at the pub on the other side after a late night. So this morning she just got on with the jobs around the house and waited for him to return. Through the window she could see the little'un from the Flag running across to her. He often came with telephone messages. Customers would ring ahead to let them know that they needed a ferry when the road across the wash was flooded.

She was surprised when she saw his dad coming after him too. Especially when his dad reached across and caught him with the flat of his hand, making him stop. Well that was a surprise, the land lord would have usually been too busy in the pub. Then Betty saw his wife, the landlady, chasing after him; apron and skirt flying as she ran along the top of the bank. The wife stopped quickly as she ran alongside her youngest, she too gave him a little slap with her hand and then carried on chasing after her husband.

When she saw Betty she cried out with an awful wail and pulled her apron over her head and stepped in behind her husband. Betty knew there was something terribly wrong. The landlord of the Flag told Betty that the ferryboat had been found in the reeds not far from the George and Dragon. There was no sign of Sam. Shortly after Sam had left the police officer at the jetty there had been a surge and the banks of the Ouse Washes had breached. The landlord held Betty by the wrists, he told her how sorry he was to bring this news. He looked into her eyes and then held her hand, she could be sure they'd do everything they could to help out.

Silence. Just the lapping of the water. And the call of birds. The wind had gone. Sam opened his eyes and found that he was face down on the side of the bank. His body was in the water but his head was resting on rough tufts of grass. His mouth tasted as if it was full of mud. Christ, it was full of mud, but only for a while. With a retch that seemed to pull down to his boots his stomach cleared the mud and water that had lain in his stomach. The watery mud and grass slime was coughed up. For a moment he felt exhausted, not really any the better for ridding himself of the slub and weeds he'd swallowed when fighting to swim out across the flood. That was last night and it was daylight now.

He was cold. Bitterly cold, he could hardly feel his legs or hands. He summoned his legs to push him up and out of the water. Somewhere, miles away, his legs responded. It was a feeble movement but it did move him forward. He suddenly felt an overwhelming love for his legs. He'd always been too busy to think about himself. Working, even when he was at school and since he'd taken over the business he hadn't really thought much about himself. He had to do; that was all. Now he wanted to save himself, realizing just how much he loved himself and life with it. His hands scrabbled to grasp at clumps of grass as his legs kicked. Joyful love. He was moving up the bank, out of the water and up to the summit.

Once he was on the top of the bank he allowed himself time to look around. The wash behind him was strangely empty. Instead of the water churning and pulling around, there was vegetation. It was slick and muddy from where, only a day before, it had been under water but now the water had gone. Sam looked out across to the farmland. The water that should have been in the wash lay glinting and shimmering, covering the black land. The water stretched for miles, across the flat fields to the horizon. Roofs of houses and barns poked out from the water, only the upper windows could be seen. Beneath the water the doors to the houses, and the lower windows, were hidden. There were no residents.

A tarmac road ran along the side of the bank. It was higher than the land below it. A distance away, a few miles, there were trucks moving. The brown camouflaged vehicles he remembered from the war. The Army must have been out to take all the people away to safety.

There was a house a short distance from Sam. It stood a little higher than other buildings he could see so the water only came half way up the front door. After struggling out of his heavy oilskin cape he hung it on a gatepost. Heaven only knew how he'd been able to stay afloat with that on him. The boots were gone, along with his socks, he walked bare foot across the road and into the farmyard. The door to the house resisted at first as he tried to open it, then the water that had backed up behind it found a way to escape and came pouring out past him. The water level must have fallen, leaving the water higher in the building. Once the two different depths stabilised he was able to open the door and wade into the front room.

In the kitchen he opened one of the two internal doors. It led into the pantry. Here he found a bottle of milk. He drank from that and then went to try the second door. As he'd expected it led to a staircase. He climbed up the steep stairway which led directly into one bedroom. There was another door which led to a larger room with a larger bed made up with blankets and a flower embroidered eiderdown. Sam took off his remaining wet clothes, pulled back the sheets and with no more thought climbed in and fell asleep.

When he woke he knew that he must get home. With no-one near him, and no vehicles, he was going to have to walk. He found a suit in the wardrobe that fitted well enough, and a pair of boots. When he went downstairs he checked the larder again. There was no more milk but there were two bottles of beer. There might be a lot of water around but he didn't fancy drinking it. He opened one of the beers and took a large gulp from it, and then he took a handful of bread and a large slice of cheese. Forcing this into his mouth he took the second bottle of beer and walked from the farmhouse.

He carried the boots as he waded across the yard and up to the road. There he put on the boots, slipped under the wire fence that separated the road from the bank and walked up to the top of the slope. Now he could see the road and the washes. On both sides the water shone in the sunlight. Over the fields that stretched away on the left the water was grey, choppy with the currents that ebbed and flowed under the surface. On the wash side the rivulets of water were still and black. There was no water of any depth across the washes. Once he got home there'd be no work rowing the ferry across. As he watched, a flock of plovers with their flashing pied plumage flew across heading for the sea of water that now covered the fenland fields. They joined the ducks and geese already settled there. His second line of income, wildfowling, wasn't going to be very lucrative either. No more cycling to the station with bags of plovers, ducks and geese for sale to London restaurants. Not for now anyway. He looked along the tarmac road and thought; if anything, or anyone, comes along I'll see them. In the meantime, with no sign of a lift and despite the badly fitting shoes, he needed to walk home, quick sharp.

Betty was sitting outside the door to her cottage. It was approaching twenty-four hours since Sam had left to row the policeman across the causeway. She was savouring the unexpected late afternoon sunshine, trying to keep her mind calm. She could see a figure walking towards her along the bank. As the man drew near she recognised him as the policeman who had instructed Sam to row him across the flood.

'Good evening madam.'

Betty wasn't inclined to reply, she nodded her head towards the police officer.

'I've come to update you on the search for your husband.'

The police officer explained that the search parties were still looking for Sam. Be assured they would continue to look for him. Betty wondered how they could find him if he'd been swept to sea, past Denver and Kings Lynn and out into the Wash.

'We might have to inform the coroner.'

The words froze Betty's heart. She looked at the police officer whose mouth continued moving, explaining the intricacies of the procedures. She didn't care about time lapse, or square miles searched, she wanted Sam back. After the police officer had left her eldest came to put an arm around her.

'Don't worry Mam,' he said. 'I'll keep the ferry going for you.'

Betty could see the care in her boy's eyes. She knew he would do it too, but she wanted him to stay on at school, not be working to help the family out. At least for now he wouldn't have to, as the causeway was open, what with the flood water spilling out onto the farm land.

With tears in her eyes she pulled her cardigan around her shoulders. It was getting cold and she needed to be getting in, it was already three o'clock and the winter afternoon was turning to evening. She looked over to the cottage where her parents-in-law now lived, since moving from the ferry cottage. She could see her mother-in-law outside, taking in the last of the daylight. Further along she could see the bridge that left the village and marked the start of the causeway.

In the darkening light of the evening she could see someone walking across the bridge. Now that the causeway was open there would be men walking across to the Flag for a drink. Then the figure turned down by the bank towards the cottage. He was walking slowly, painfully. A tired man, exhausted. Betty looked again and recognised her husband. She gave a loud shout and started running along the bank to him. Her eldest son swept past her, arms outstretched, shouting to his Daddy. Across the river she could see her mother-in-law similarly running and her father-in-law hobbling behind her, shouting too.

Sam held his arms out to them as they ran to greet him. It might be cruel that the ferry and the wildfowling money would be lost, but he had his family. And for now that was all the riches he needed.

Author's note

Dear reader, thank you for reading my stories. I hope you have enjoyed the collection. My stories have been inspired by the Fens and East Anglia. Some of these stories have had success in competitions. I have a novel nearing completion that will continue with the themes from these stories. Please look out for its release. All of the stories are fiction and are drawn from my imagination.

Three articles previously published in the magazine *'Practical Poultry'* follow. These recount my experiences as a hen keeper and the great happiness I had as the owner of a very special cockerel, Napoleon.

Nothing to crow about

'What you need,' said my husband, 'is a cockerel. That will keep the hens in order.'

Oh right, I thought, how sexist can that be. As if women need a man about to keep everything peaceful. The next day saw us visit our favourite chicken breeder, Tony, looking for another Maran hen. Going round the corner to his pens we saw the most fabulous cockerel.

'That's the Lace Winged Wyandotte I told you about,' I said to my husband.

'No it ain't,' said Tony. 'That's a Marans, that is.' He was beautiful and I said so. 'You can have 'im if you like,' replied Tony. So we did.

My neighbour was quick to come over and inspect him once he'd arrived. She admired his tail feathers and commented on the way they were already growing into a proud arch. I held him and stroked the back of his head as we chatted. I knew she'd had difficulty with her own cockerel, he had clawed at the back of her legs and left her fearful to enter his pen. I decided that I would handle this cockerel as much as possible to try to encourage good behaviour from him.

Napoleon, as we called him, loved his hens. He would cluck to them when I sprinkled hen treat in the run and would share the grains with them, waiting while they took their pick. At night he would escort any late hens to bed, even coming out again one evening when hens in another pen caused a commotion through being late to bed. Their own, neglectful, cockerel stayed firmly in his house.

With his plumage growing sleek and silky his tail, as my neighbour had predicted, grew full and arched in layered curves. The grey down around the back of his legs grew soft and fluffy. His neck feathers lay glossy and fluid over his shoulders. Napoleon was a beautiful bird. As can happen with Marans he did suffer a little from scaly leg mite, so we kept on top of this, regularly picking him up for treatment. At the same time I would stroke the back of his head, admiring his shiny feathers.

My hen owning neighbour came over at times to discuss his progress. I raised the subject of his crowing, did she think the other neighbours would be disturbed.

'No', she replied, 'they sleep at the back of the house. If they can put up with my cockerels they'll put up with yours.' I didn't think to ask her if the noise would be a problem to her, hardly likely for someone who lived with so many cockerels of her own.

After we'd had Napoleon for three or four months I met a self-sufficiency group at a village show. We discussed raising chicks. I hadn't thought about it before, but it all seemed so easy. I could follow their guidance and in time have either more hens (and eventually eggs) or lovely roast dinners. It was too late that year to raise a brood but I started to plan for the following season.

Early the next Spring I picked up a magazine and discovered that if I was going to raise any birds I should be incubating right then, with a view to hatchings in April. I mentioned this to a friend who was often passing by walking his dog. He told me he'd try and find me a broody hen. I collected the eggs but the broody failed to appear. I contacted the hen keeping neighbour and asked if she had any space in her incubator as I'd collected so many eggs. She was more than happy to take all sixteen.

I collected a second batch but again the broody failed to appear.

'What you want to do,' said my dog walking friend, 'is sell them eggs. I'll see if I can get a broody for you next week if you start saving another lot.' I pointed out that I didn't like to sell eggs as this would be undermining the sales of my hen owning neighbour. 'Oh, she hasn't had any eggs for ages,' my dog walking friend assured me.

The neighbour didn't take well to my selling eggs. She sent me a message via Facebook in which she outlined the many transgressions I had made against the law by selling the dozen. Chastised, I apologised, promised not to do this again, and ordered an incubator for immediate dispatch.

The question, over whether Napoleon was fertile or not, was answered three weeks later when our chicks started to arrive. Supported by a handbook and the incubator manual we successfully hatched out our first brood. We went for a second batch. These were even more successful and in this brood I had Maran cross Light Sussex as well as pure Maran. We'd been uncertain about the fertility of the eggs as my neighbour had informed me that only two eggs of the sixteen I'd given her had hatched, and these had both died.

In the first batch we'd included six Lavender Leghorn hatching eggs, bought on e-bay. The Leghorns raced and flew around the brooder and the Marans watched in amazement while the Leghorns whirled, like dervishes, around them. The second batch were a far sweeter bunch as we'd included six Golden Silkie eggs. Three of these hatched. One was tiny, as it arrived a full day after all the other chicks. I came down at three in the morning to check its progress, having gone to bed while the first breaks were appearing in the egg. When it hatched the chick went into turbo charged reverse. I worried at the prospects for this one. However, by the next morning he (or she) had found forward gear and was pushing his diminutive little self into the centre of the brood.

It was about this time that my hen owning neighbour started to complain about Napoleon's crowing. At first we made the mistake of not taking her seriously as she had cockerels of her own. It was quite hard for us to be able to tell whose cockerel was crowing outside and it did seem as though her cockerels were the first to rise in the morning. My neighbour then moved her chicken runs to the far side of her garden, and reported us to the Environmental Health Officer. I can't begin to explain to you how quickly this all happened. Within a few weeks my neighbour had gone from collecting my eggs for incubation, with no mention of noise, to putting in a complaint to the council.

Trying to sort out a cockerel crowing problem with short notice is a difficult thing to do. The problem is that a living animal is involved. Fair enough cockerels can quickly go in a pot for dinner, but we couldn't see that this was right for him. I contacted the EHO and requested advice, this was declined as the official was of the opinion that common sense was the best thing in cases like this. Distraught at the unexpected threat that suddenly faced Napoleon I found it difficult to think where common sense had been applied.

I suggested to my husband that he build me a new run next to the house and he did this for me. Having only weekends it was not possible to move the cockerel immediately and so the messages on Facebook started to arrive...

'Could you put the cockerel in a box at night'…….. 'Could you try putting a sock over his head'….. 'I've found on the internet that if you hang a pole across the house he'll not be able to lift his head, so won't be able to crow'.

To top it all a colleague at work suggested that I should have the cockerel's voice-box removed. And all this time the beautiful boy continued to sunbathe with his wives, to share his dust bath and chicken treats. At night he escorted his girls to the safety of their house. I didn't like to tell him what was going on or in any way let him know that this idyll was coming to an end.

Finally I felt I'd had enough. I told my dog walking friend that I needed to find a new home for Napoleon.

'Oh, I'll have him,' he said.

'But you've got neighbours too,' I said, anxious to avoid a continuous cycle of complaints leading to re-homings for the cockerel. Truth to tell though, I did feel that we were probably the only house in the village that would be unable to keep a cockerel. We live in rural Norfolk after all, there couldn't be many people likely to complain.

So that's how this part of the story ends. My friend came round with a cat box, I caught Napoleon, who rested comfortably in my arms expecting a cuddle, and then I put him through the small door of the box. With no trouble, no fuss, he went in and turned to make himself more comfortable in the straw. I could see his sleek feathers, his lovely barred plumage and then he was gone.

Later that day I visited the hen run, now quiet and feeling empty. The girls seemed to be having difficulty working out what to do on their own. There were small scuffles as they established a new order. There was a vacuum where Napoleon had once been, and I felt it too.

The Comeback King!

The cockerel was back. My neighbour had complained about his crowing and a friend, who often walked his dog past our cottage, had taken him away for a few weeks. Now the dog-walking friend had brought the cockerel back. Not because of his neighbours but because his hens were complaining. Napoleon, the cockerel, was used to chasing and treading his hens first thing in the morning. The hens at his new home had been outraged at his demands. They were pampered ladies and they ran from Napoleon. When his attentions still proved too much for them, they went off lay, so my dog walking friend put Napoleon in a pen on his own while we built a new run. As soon as it was ready Napoleon returned.

When I got the news that Napoleon was coming home I called the local council's Environmental Health Officer (EHO). The EHO was extremely helpful. We had previously exchanged emails about the cockerel noise and it hadn't seemed as if hc was able to offer any guidance to me. Speaking to him I now found he had a lot of useful information to provide and that he was supportive and positive in his comments. I explained that the cockerel would be going into a pen at least 50 metres from the neighbour's house and described the arrangements we had made for the enclosure. He advised that, for prosecution to proceed, the noise levels in my neighbour's house would have to reach 90 decibels. As an example, he explained, human speech is about 70 decibels. I now felt able to make an informed decision about keeping Napoleon.

We had moved some young cockerels into the run before Napoleon arrived. These were mainly Marans, the result of the first two hatchings we'd had in the spring.

There were also three Lavender Leghorns. Out of six Leghorn hatching eggs I'd bought on eBay, I'd hatched three cockerels and one hen. The eggs had cost £16 but I was happy that the hen, a beautiful sleek black bird, was worth the price. In total I now had about fifteen cockerels and twelve hens. I hadn't expected such a large number of cockerels, but here I was with fifteen, all primed to start crowing within a few weeks.

As soon as Napoleon moved in with the youngsters he made it clear that he intended to be boss and chased them around the pen for a while, before taking a break to crow a little and eat more food. We would normally have introduced a new bird when the others were roosting but this wasn't necessary for Napoleon. It was best to let the youngsters know right away that the big bird was back. He soon took to sunbathing with the young birds and, although he would chase them around the pen, he never showed any real aggression.

His enclosure was under our bedroom window but I heard very little of him. In the early summer, before my neighbour's complaints, I had loved the sound of his crowing. Now the sound brought only feelings of guilt. His call wasn't particularly loud if heard from our drive which was half way between the neighbour and the cockerel pen. I calculated the sound there was easily only that of human speech levels, not reaching the 90 decibels that would bring action from the council, but that was just half of the argument. I already knew from the EHO that prosecution wasn't really on the agenda but finding a way to live alongside the neighbour was.

When I was letting the cockerels out one morning a strange sound came from inside the poultry house. It was an unusual cry, as if a cough had formed into a call. The birds emerging through the pop-hole scattered in alarm. Then one of the young birds came to the hatch, opened its mouth, and the same sound rang out. The bird himself looked surprised. When he repeated the sound he looked pleased. It wasn't a good sound as far as I was concerned. It meant that time was nearly up for these youngsters.

I had decided that raising our own birds for meat was acceptable as I'd be able to offer a better quality of life to my birds than many are offered in a commercial setting. If you'd asked me at the start of the season how many cockerels I would have I'd have said, 'maybe four or five, plenty for roast dinners'. In reality I had more cockerels than hens, and rehoming through the free ads was never going to be an option. A quick humane killing, then straight to the freezer, was the only future for these birds. If I couldn't eat their meat, I told myself, I would have to become vegetarian. It would be hypocritical otherwise. And eating eggs would be questionable as for every egg laying hen there is a cockerel hatched, and I expect many of those are killed at day old in a commercial setting. It's a hard fact of life, and now I needed to make sure that the end of these cockerel's lives would be managed as carefully and kindly as any other part of the time they'd had here at my cottage.

I'd been looking at humane ways of killing the cockerels and had learnt about different forms of equipment that are available. When I checked on the internet I found the prices started at £600, too much for a small number of cockerels. I spoke to a friend who is a university professor in forensics; I knew he would probably have experienced culling animals in his career. He confirmed that he had and that he could cull the birds for me. I asked him if it would be humane, yes, said the professor, but probably not legal. I didn't ask for any more details and let the conversation go in a different direction. My husband was confident that he could do the job but I had a fear of the cockerel's death not being quick. It wasn't quite the time to start learning how to do something like this without skilled help.

I did know someone who had the experience to carry out the culling for me. I hadn't approached him earlier as I knew he would not be keen. A former shooting man who had always lived in the country, my friend had been able to kill poultry from a young age. He had some forty years' experience. Of all the options I had looked at I knew this was the best way for the cockerels to go.

I rang his wife and asked if he would be likely to do this for me. 'Well,' she said, 'I think he's gone a bit soft with age, he doesn't like doing it now.'

'I know,' I replied, 'would you ask him if he'll do it for me?'

He rang back and replied that he would.

My friend arrived the following Sunday. It was mid-September and the birds were now about nineteen weeks old. He joked when he arrived saying he'd wondered if he should bring a cape and scythe, I also laughed but more nervously. I'd woken that morning listening to the cockerels crowing. There were a few different calls now. I always knew Napoleon. His call was like a creaking door, a kind of cock- a-squawk, it had never been melodious. Some others were a bit more tuneful, they had been improving with practice. Then amongst them I heard a new call, a fluting cry, with pitch perfect notes. I imagined the young bird in his house wondering at the special sound he had made. He'd managed a beautiful, balanced call, and now, because of that, this day was going to be his last.

'Right, get me one of those birds then, 'said my Grim Reaper friend. 'And don't let any of them others know what's going on or they'll go crazy and we won't get anything done.'

I walked into the pen with my husband and watched him select a cockerel. He carried it away to the side of the house, I heard a flutter of wings, then nothing. Husband came back and I selected another bird for him. Each bird was carried away and I would hear a flutter of wings, then nothing, and my husband would return for another bird. The cockerels were by now back at the feeder undisturbed by anything that was going on. I picked up one of the cockerels to hand to my husband but he picked another bird and told me to just hang on to the one I had until he got back. I held the cockerel in the crook of my arm while we waited, and stroked the back of his neck. He turned his head to look at me. He knew me but I didn't know which cockerel this was. He was one I would have hatched and put under the heat lamp to dry out, in the brooder he would have made his first attempts to eat chick crumb, later he would have nestled up to the other chicks. Unlike male birds culled at day old he'd had a summer living in a pen on the lawn and there he pecked at grass and perched in the sun with his companions. More recently he'd been part of the flock living happily in this pen, spending his days in the company of birds he'd known from the very start. I put him down not knowing if my husband would pick him up next, whether he would be in this culling, or if he would make it through to another day. The feeling of the soft feathers on the back of his neck, and the way he relaxed while I held him in my arms, stayed with me for the rest of the day.

'That's about it then,' said my husband after a couple more cockerels had gone. 'We'll leave those others. They can stay until Christmas.' I went round to look at the now dead cockerels. There they were, hanging, heads down, eyes closed.

'It looks a neat job,' I congratulated my Grim Reaper friend. He was pleased at my comment. 'Yeah,' he said, 'they all went well, just a quick click, killed straight away.'

My husband spent the afternoon preparing the birds and by the evening I had the portions packed and into the freezer. Next morning Napoleon's call woke me at six, which is when I need to get up so that I can feed and water all the animals before going to work. As usual I didn't hear him call any earlier, just when it was time for me to get up. Then there was another call and my heart sank, still more noise nuisance to worry about. This crow rang out, a tuneful, fluting call. It was the cockerel from the day before, with his gift to this world, a perfect musical cry of 'cock-a-doodle-doo'.

Mixed Fortunes

It's a golden September day that feels more like October, the season is sliding into autumn. We're dusting the hens with lice powder and covering their legs with mite cream. I cradle each hen like a baby while husband lifts both wings and dusts underneath and fluffs the powder around their bottoms. Then he smears the leg mite cream around their legs. After each hen the layers of powder and ointment build up on his hands. I have powder and patches of ointment smeared across my jumper.

'It's a good job we only have eight hens to do,' I say to husband. 'We'd be here all day if we had more.'

There are experiences, like holidays, where your mind re-visits every so often and basks in the enjoyment of the event. And experiences where the only good thing that can be said is that, in time, this will be nothing, it will all be forgotten. My experience of raising poultry from fertile eggs falls towards the latter. When a member of the local sustainability group told to me about raising young chicks he said that some would be cockerels, so, excellent for roast dinners; and some would be hens, good for laying eggs. He didn't mention the noise nuisance of young cockerels crowing. A lot of my chicks turned out to be noisy males, and the last straw was when two Silkies, from bought eggs, started to crow. By the end of my first season I counted that from three incubations of Marans, Leghorns and Silkies, I had raised about twenty cockerels and only ten hens.

Anyway, back to the present. The pen we're in at the moment contains eight Marans and another two Light Sussex are in the back garden. We moved them there when one of the Light Sussex went to live under the hen house after being bullied by the Marans so we took her and another Light Sussex and put them round the back with the soft fruit. Those two hens got along happily until one died.

'Leave that one there on her own,' said husband, 'the other Light Sussex in the Marans pen has paired up with the cross, they're quite happy together.'

But the Light Sussex left on her own was not happy. Within a couple of days she'd taken to her house and wasn't coming out. I thought she'd die if I didn't get her a companion. Plan 'A' had been to get a little Silkie hen to keep her happy but I didn't feel there was time. One evening I took the remaining Light Sussex from the Marans pen and put her in the house with the lonely hen. I could hear cluckings of relief and delight from inside. The two old friends were back together, they knew each other well.

I took the decision to keep the Light Sussex cross Marans in the pen with the pure bred Marans. She was more flighty than the older Sussex hens and I thought there would be problems and that she might fly over to the neighbour's garden. In any case she had been raised with the Marans and seemed to be quite happy with them. I was of the opinion that the Light Sussex had been keeping close to the cross, which was a white hen, rather than the cross keeping close to the Sussex. Sadly the white cross died in the summer. I'll never know if my decision was the cause or if it would just have happened anyway.

We'd aimed for twenty hens as the house and run was plenty big enough and we'd hoped to make money from egg sales to boost our income. I'd read the local authority website for guidance on the law for selling eggs, not wishing to do anything illegal. All I could find was that recycled boxes must not be used and that the (new) egg-boxes should be dated. The best before date for the eggs can be up to four weeks from laying. I have a Level Three Certificate in Food Hygiene, (Distinction), so I understand the reasons for these requirements. The use of second hand boxes would invite cross contamination, boxes would go from one kitchen where bacteria could be collected, to another. Who would want to think of putting a box in their fridge that might have sat in some-one else's messy kitchen? The other area the law is concerned about is selling in date, this is where the best before date is important. When I box up my eggs I make a note of the best before date of the first egg placed in the box. Any eggs put into the box after that first egg will certainly be in date as I will have allowed a shorter best before date than required, which is 28 days. I did look at buying pre-printed labels but found them expensive so I designed my own on my computer and printed them on labels bought through eBay. For an illustration I chose a photo of my hens with the cockerel I had until last year.

The cockerel, Napoleon, had to go after a neighbour complained about the noise. For a few weeks he was kept in a separate pen, as far away as possible from the neighbour's house. He spent most of that time sitting in the corner of the run that was nearest to his ladies. Then Wood Green Animal Sanctuary offered him a place, after he'd been on the waiting list for most of the summer. On the day when it came for him to leave I caught him up in a cat box and carried him out of the garden gate, past his hens. As he went he clucked to the ladies, calling to them as his favourites, not knowing he wasn't to see them again.

At Wood Green the assistant was very kind, I completed the paperwork to hand Napoleon over and then we took him to a stable to meet his new friends. He'd been provided with some female companions already, three ISA Brown hens and three Golden Sebright. I opened the cat box for him but he stayed firmly wedged, refusing to come out. There was no room for him to turn so I gently pulled his legs out and tilted the box on edge a little, hoping he would fall out. Still he wouldn't move, he appeared to be holding on with his wings.

'He's nervous about his new home,' said the assistant.

I gave the box a bit of a shake and gradually the bird fell out. As soon as he touched the floor he ran to the other side of the stable, furthest from us.

'Oooh, he's big,' said the assistant. The Sebrights were clearly thinking the same thing.

Napoleon did his 'Ali Shuffle', working out what to do next. There was some wheat in a feeder so I threw a handful over to him. He clucked with pleasure and started to peck at the food. After a moment he looked up to check the surroundings again. His hens were looking a bit apprehensive, being rescue hens they'd probably never seen a cockerel in full plume before, but he seemed to think they might be alright.

Now we just have these few hens, and on this glorious September day we are going to move them over to the pen where Napoleon spent those last weeks. We will turn the old run into a vegetable plot as it's sunny and open, it's also further from the house so the hens could be safer in this run. All is going well and there is just one hen to powder. As we finish with each bird we place them in the house, so by this time there is just the single hen and she knows something is up. My hens are all easy to handle, I've had them since hatching and when I approach they crouch and wait for me to pick them up.

This hen thinks otherwise, she's not sure what's going on and in the absence of any information she's keeping away from us. She runs and hides under the hen house which is raised up from the ground by about six inches. We get a broom handle and gently guide her out so then she runs to the back of the house where it is close to the edge of the fence. We can't follow her down there so husband walks to the far side and I wait for him to shoo her through to me. Only husband forgets the low eaves of the hen-house and bangs his head on the sharp fascia board he's not pleased, shouts and swears pulling at the board as he does so. This does nothing to calm the hen who makes a break past me and heads back to the space under the hen house. We get the broom handle out.

This time when we guide her out I manage to catch her. She's confused about everything by now and is ready to give up. I cradle her like a baby, we fluff powder around her bottom and off she goes to join the others. In no time they're in their new run. They have the left over brassicas the cabbage whites attacked earlier in the summer to pick around at together with the old runner beans we grew in the run. They'll be fine there and we'll let the flock naturally reduce in size until we can maintain it at about four or five hens. After all the angst of crowing cockerels and losing hens, I've decided, my days as an egg producer are over.

ABOUT THE AUTHOR

Lisa lives in rural Norfolk with her five cocker spaniels, two cats and three hens.

She has a degree in English Literature and Creative Writing. When not writing Lisa works as a lecturer at a local college.

Printed in Great Britain
by Amazon